# LET'S PLAY
# TAG!

 Read the Page

 Read the Story

 Game

 Repeat

 Stop

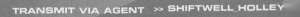

DESTINATION

TOKYO, JAPAN

Disney · PIXAR

*Cars*

2

# PROJECT
# UNDERCOVER

ILLUSTRATED BY ESTUDI IBOIX

JAPAN

Mater was excited. He was travelling with his best buddy Lightning McQueen in the World Grand Prix. First stop: Tokyo, Japan.

"Boy, this place sure is different," Mater said.

Mater didn't fit in so well in Japan. By mistake, he disturbed a Zen master.

He confused wasabi for ice cream!

4

And he sprang an oil leak!

Lightning was embarrassed. "Mater, you have to get a hold of yourself. You're making a scene!"

During the first race, Mater spotted some cars down an alley. "Wow! A live karate demonstration! Give 'em a right! Now a left! Left, right, left!"

Lightning heard Mater over the intercom and thought he was giving driving instructions.

Lightning got confused!

"Mater, I lost because of you!" he said angrily.

"This is exactly why I don't bring you along to these things!"

Mater offered to talk to the race officials, "Maybe if I explained what happened, it could help."

"I don't need your help!" replied Lightning as he drove off.

Mater was sad and decided to head home. He didn't want to mess up any more of Lightning's races.

Little did Mater know that two secret agents, Finn McMissile and Holley Shiftwell, had been watching him.

They thought Mater was an American spy disguised as a tow truck! They grabbed Mater before he could leave.

Holley showed Mater a picture of an engine she and Finn couldn't identify. Mater knew exactly what it was. "That's one of the worst engines ever made. But those replacement parts are original. They ain't easy to come by."

"Rare parts! That's the clue we've been looking for!" Holley said gratefully.

Finn and Holley thought they could use Mater's help, so Mater went with them on their mission—a trip to Paris to meet with an informant.

In Paris, the informant told the spies that the bad guys were planning a secret meeting in Italy.

"We've got to find a way to infiltrate that meeting and find out what's going on," said Holley.

FRANCE

On the train to Italy, Mater
agreed to go undercover.

Holley gave Mater special spy gear and a computer
that created disguises.

Meanwhile, Lightning McQueen was in Italy
preparing for the next race. Luigi introduced Lightning
to his uncle, Topolino.

Uncle Topolino told Lightning a story about two friends
who fought all the time, but in the end, were always there
for each other. It reminded Lightning of Mater.

"Mater's always been there for me, too." He wished
he could tell Mater he was sorry.

The next day, Mater disguised himself as one
of the bad guys. He slipped into the secret
meeting and heard the evildoers say they
were sabotaging the World Grand Prix!
A criminal named Professor Z was going to eliminate
Lightning McQueen at the final race in London.

"Oh no! I gotta warn him!"
thought Mater.

But before Mater could reach Lightning, Professor Z and his crew captured Mater, Finn, and Holley!

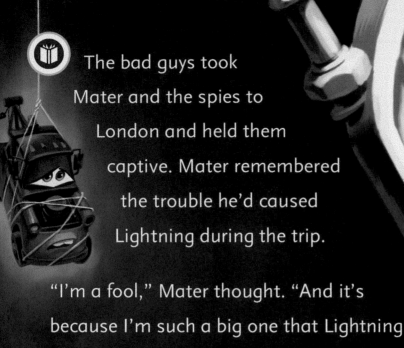

The bad guys took Mater and the spies to London and held them captive. Mater remembered the trouble he'd caused Lightning during the trip.

"I'm a fool," Mater thought. "And it's because I'm such a big one that Lightning is gonna get hurt."

Mater was determined to save his friend, and he escaped!

Finn and Holley soon followed.

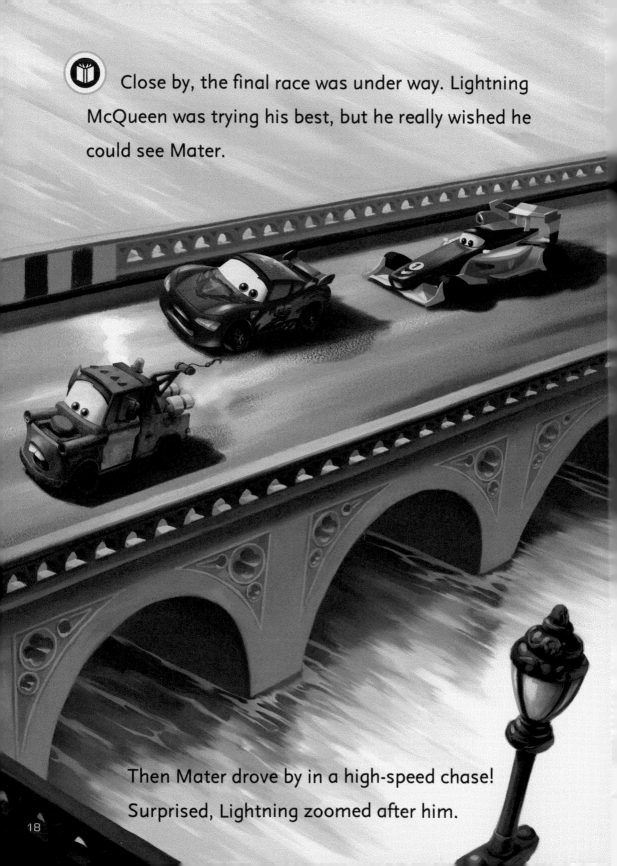

Close by, the final race was under way. Lightning McQueen was trying his best, but he really wished he could see Mater.

Then Mater drove by in a high-speed chase! Surprised, Lightning zoomed after him.

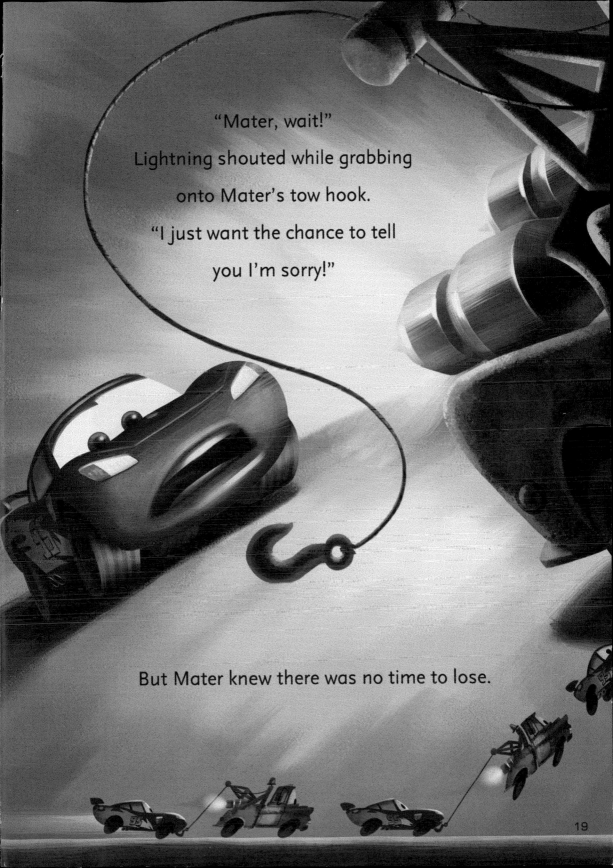

"Mater, wait!"
Lightning shouted while grabbing
onto Mater's tow hook.
"I just want the chance to tell
you I'm sorry!"

But Mater knew there was no time to lose.

With some quick thinking, Mater helped the spies stop the evil plot, and captured Professor Z.

The day was saved!

"Thank you for your help," Holley told Mater. "You may not be a spy, but you're the smartest, most honest gentleman we've ever met."

Lightning was glad to finally have a chance to talk to his friend. "Sorry I was so hard on you, Mater."

"And I'm sorry I kept messing stuff up," Mater replied.

At last, the two friends were together again.

It was the end of the World Grand Prix, and both Mater and Lightning felt like winners.

Hello   Goodbye   1, 2, 3

Please   Thank You

I am speed.